P9-BIK-369

THE OLD MOTEL MYSTERY

created by
GERTRUDE CHANDLER WARNER

Illustrated by Charles Tang

ALBERT WHITMAN & Company
Morton Grove, Illinois

ISBN 0-8075-5966-0

13

Printed in the U.S.A.

Contents

CHAPTER 1

The Old Motel

Aunt Jane and the four Alden children, Violet, Benny, Henry, and Jessie, hurried out of the Miami Airport. They had arrived in Florida to visit Aunt Jane's friend, Kay Kingsley.

Grandfather's sister, Aunt Jane said, "Hurry, children." She smiled to herself. She was lucky to have married a man like Andy Bean. He was most understanding and had urged her to visit her friend and stay as long as she liked. Grandfather Alden had agreed that she take her nieces and nephews with her for a Florida vacation.

As they came out into the hot August sunshine, Jessie said, "I miss Watch already."

"Oh, our dog is happy keeping Grandfather Alden company," Henry reassured her. "You wouldn't want Grandfather to be all alone, would you?"

Jessie shook her head, but she felt sad.

"Look!" Benny shouted. "Palm trees!"

Aunt Jane laughed. "You'll see stranger sights than palm trees in the Florida Everglades," she said.

Benny squinted up at her. "What are the Everglades?" he asked.

"The Everglades are a huge national park in Florida. The park has lots of waterways and swamps with all kinds of wildlife, from alligators to pelicans," Violet said. "I've read about it."

Henry grinned. "Just wait until we see it."

Benny's round face lit up, and his eyes grew big. "Alligators?"

"Alligators," Henry echoed. "You might not see one, though, because there are not as many now as there used to be."

Jessie hurried forward. "That must be Kay Kingsley in the blue dress. She's hugging Aunt Jane."

The four of them ran forward.

Kay Kingsley stopped talking. Her dark eyes admired the four Aldens lined up in front of her. "Jane! Are these the Alden children?"

Aunt Jane smiled proudly. "Yes, indeed." She placed her hands on Benny's shoulders. "This is Benny, the youngest."

"I'm six years old," he said proudly.

Aunt Jane touched him under the chin. "So you are, Benny." She motioned the others forward. "This is Henry, the oldest."

Politely, Henry shook Mrs. Kingsley's hand. He was fourteen years old, of medium height with brown hair.

"This is Violet," Aunt Jane continued. "She's ten, and as you can see, she loves the color of her name."

Violet's face turned pink, but she smiled when she glanced down at her lavender T-shirt. Shyly, she said, "Hello, Mrs. Kingsley."

Kay chuckled. "Please. Call me Kay."

"And last but not least," Aunt Jane said, stepping to one side and drawing Jessie forward, "this is Jessie Alden. She's twelve."

Jessie's eyes twinkled. "Hello, Kay." A blue ribbon tied back her brown hair.

"Jane, I have so much to tell you," Kay said happily, putting her arm around her friend. "All of you," she ordered pleasantly, glancing back, "follow me!"

Kay, her blue skirt rustling slightly in the warm breeze, walked to a white van. She opened the driver's side and paused. "Oh, Jane, it's so good to see you and these darling children." There was a catch in her throat. "I was lonely in my empty motel."

Jane gave her a quick look. Kay sounded as if she really needed someone. "Is your motel empty?" She couldn't hide the surprise in her voice.

"Almost," Kay answered. "Out of ten units I only have two rented." She slid into the driver's seat. "But you'll soon see for yourself."

The Aldens couldn't wait to see the motel

and the swimming pool and the tennis court they'd heard Aunt Jane talk about.

The ride to the motel was fun. The children's eyes were glued to the tall cypress trees and the marshy grass. In the distance long fingers of water, dotted with clumps of reeds, reached into the mangrove forests.

Cranes screeched as they walked along the marsh on skinny legs. Peering into the muddy water, the big birds waited for a fish to appear.

"Florida is sure different from Greenfield," Benny said.

Violet laughed. "You're not lonesome, are you, Benny?"

"Not me," Benny said firmly.

After a forty-mile ride, Kay arrived in the small town of Lyndale. She drove a few more miles until she came to a narrow lane that led to her motel. Large cypress trees shaded both sides of the road. When the car stopped, the Aldens glimpsed a long building nestled among the trees, but it didn't look very inviting. The motel, a dark brown, had peeling paint and a roof with missing shingles. One

door hung from its hinges and a few of the windowpanes were broken. All in all it was a pretty gloomy sight.

"Is that the motel?" Benny asked, wrinkling his nose.

"That's my Cypress Motel," Kay said sadly. She realized the bad shape it was in. "I inherited the motel a number of years ago. It wasn't in great shape then, and I guess I've let it get even worse. I just didn't want to put much money in it. However," she said in a more cheerful tone, "the white house on the hill is where I live. There's room for all of us. Unless," she hesitated, "you children would rather stay in one of the motel units. There's a kitchenette," she added.

"Oh, we want to stay in the motel," Jessie said, not hesitating a second.

"Right," Henry agreed. "We're used to taking care of ourselves. Aren't we?"

"Yes, we are!" Benny and Violet said together.

"Then Jane and I will stay in the house and you children will be on your own. Of course, you'll have dinner with us tonight.

Next to the end unit is a bicycle shed with all sizes of bikes. You can choose one that you like." Kay looked at Jane. "Is that satisfactory?"

"Oh, my, yes," Jane answered. "The four of them like to be independent."

"Where's the pool?" Benny asked, wiping his forehead. "It's hot."

"I'm sorry," Kay answered. "The pool is empty. It needs a good cleaning before being filled with water."

"Cleaning. That's where we come in," Violet said with a smile.

Henry glanced around. Even the tennis court was overgrown with weeds and vines. But it was a lovely place, he thought. Kay's white house stood on the hill, and the motel was at the foot of it. The cypress trees and the crooked lane leading to it all added to the Cypress Motel's charm. It was too bad that it was so run-down.

CHAPTER 2

The Empty Swimming Pool

Kay parked the van before her charming white house with a picket fence around it. The car had barely stopped when the children scrambled out.

All at once they noticed a tall, black-haired man with a mustache. With his hands on his hips and his booted feet far apart, he turned to Violet and Jessie.

"May I carry your suitcases?" he asked.

"Oh, no," Henry said, stepping forward. "We'll carry them down the hill to the motel."

The man smiled. "I'll be glad to help."

"Thanks," Benny said, lifting a heavy suitcase and dropping it to the ground. His round face was red. "We can do it," he said, panting.

"This is Rolf Jensen," Kay said. "He's my right hand, always willing to help me." She then introduced him to Aunt Jane and the four Aldens.

"Hi, everyone," Rolf said. "I'm glad you could come to Florida." He glanced at Kay. "I think Kay could use a little company."

Kay hastily interrupted, as if to dismiss her troubles, "Rolf has a barge boat that takes tourists out into the Everglades."

"How about it?" Rolf said, one black eyebrow shooting upward. "Would you like a tour?" he asked the Aldens.

"Yes, yes," Benny said excitedly. "I want to see an alligator."

A grin spread across Rolf's tanned face. "Well, we'll see what we can do about that."

"In the meantime," Kay said, "come into the house. We'll have a cold glass of orange juice."

"Hmmmm, that sounds good," Violet said.

"I pick the oranges from my orange trees in the backyard," Kay said, opening the screen door.

"Oh," Jessie said, her brown eyes sparkling. "I've never seen an orange tree."

"Me neither," Benny said.

"You'll have plenty of time to explore in a little while," Aunt Jane said, smiling. She knew they'd be all over the grounds before evening.

The children entered the living room. In the corner of a small sofa, a marmalade cat was curled up.

"Oh," Benny said. "A pretty orange cat with white paws!" He rushed forward, arms extended.

Quickly the cat jumped down and ran into a corner.

Violet followed, coming close to the frightened cat. Softly she stroked its fur, and before long the cat was purring.

Kay laughed. "You've made friends with Willie."

"Willie," Henry said gently, reaching down and letting Willie smell his hand.

"Let's call Grandfather," Violet said, "and tell him we're safe."

"Oh, let's," Benny said.

So they talked to Grandfather Alden and found out he was all right, too. He said the house seemed very quiet with just Mrs. McGregor and Watch.

Kay poured the cold juice and set out a plate of cookies. When they'd finished their snack, Jessie said, "We'll be back in time for dinner."

Then, despite the heavy suitcases, they hurried down the hill, eager to see their new vacation home.

Benny was the first to reach the door on the end unit and push it open. The unit had two large rooms plus a kitchenette. After tonight they could be independent of the house on the hill. They'd do their own cooking and make out their own grocery lists.

"It's so gloomy in here," Violet said, opening the blinds.

"Isn't it?" Jessie agreed, unpacking her

jeans, shorts, and tops. "Wouldn't new drapes and a bedspread help?"

"You bet it would," Henry answered.

Benny tested the bed in the room he and Henry would share. "It bounces good," he said, laughing and jumping up and down.

Henry laughed, too. "Let's check out the motel grounds." He held the door open.

"Oh, yes," Jessie said, "lets."

Violet had walked ahead. "Oh, no," she said. Disappointed, she sank down on the grass. "Look!" She pointed to the pool.

The three Aldens hurried forward. Jessie and Benny peered over the edge of the pool.

"It's all green," Benny said. "I wish we could go swimming."

"I was hoping we could go swimming every day, too, Benny," Jessie said with a frown.

"Not with that yucky green stuff on the bottom," Benny said with a groan. "What is that?"

"Moss," Henry answered shortly. "If we scrape it off, though, there's no reason the pool can't be filled."

"Do you think Kay would do that?" Violet questioned softly.

"I'm sure she would," Jessie replied. "I just think this motel is too much of a burden for her."

"That's where we come in," Benny said, folding his arms. "I'm a good scraper."

"So am I," Henry said. "If it means we can swim, I know we'll all be good scrapers!"

"That Rolf Jensen seems like a nice fellow." Jessie looked at Violet. "Do you think he'd help us?"

"I'm sure he'll help as much as he can, but he has a job, remember?" Violet said.

"Oh, boy, he runs a barge boat." Benny grinned. "I can't wait for our tour."

Everyone laughed.

Suddenly a tall black girl, dressed in white shorts and top, appeared through the trees. When she spotted the Aldens, she halted, and her dark eyes glanced from one to the other. "You must be the Aldens," she said with a dazzling smile.

"We are," Henry said, introducing himself and the rest.

"Kay told me about you. I'm Catherine Wilson," said the beautiful girl. "I'm an anthropology student at the University of Georgia."

"An-thro-pol-ogy?" Benny said slowly with a puzzled look.

She laughed, a happy tinkling sound. "That's the 'study of man.' In this case, I'm studying the Seminole Indians who live in the Everglades."

"How thrilling!" Jessie said, unable to keep the excitement out of her voice.

"Yes, I'm just about finished with my paper," Catherine said. "I'll go back to their camp several more times. I rented a car for the month and I go back and forth in that. I drive to the edge of the Everglades where Lacota, a Seminole Indian, meets me in his boat. He takes me to their camp."

"Do you live here, Catherine?" Violet asked.

"Yes, I'm staying in unit number nine, next to Millicent."

"Millicent?" Jessie questioned, unable to keep the admiration from shining in her eyes.

Besides being a student, Jessie wondered if Catherine was also a model.

"Millicent Fair lives in the end unit number ten. She's a very nice older woman, who I'm sure you'll soon meet." Catherine had a little smile on her face as if she knew Millicent's habits quite well.

"We're staying in unit number one," Henry said. "Right now we're looking things over."

"Next to you is the bike shed. You can take out a bike anytime you want to." She smiled. "The bikes are in good condition, but everything else is pretty run-down." Catherine shook her head. "I feel sorry for Kay. She's so sweet and works so hard."

Catherine paused. "It's nice to meet you, but I'm in a bit of a hurry." Waving, she moved toward the motel. "I have to change. I'm having supper in the Seminole camp."

"Wow!" Benny said, his eyes wide. "What fun!"

"We'd better go, too." Henry said.

" 'Bye, Catherine," Violet said. "We'll see you later."

The children walked on, brushing through the thick untrimmed shrubs. When they reached the tennis court, they stopped, unable to take another step. .

"Oh, no," Jessie said, shaking her head. "The court is overgrown with vines and weeds."

"We can pull weeds." Violet said, a determined expression on her face.

"Yes, we can!" Benny shouted. "I'm a good weed puller."

"I see we have our work cut out for us," Henry said, glancing around at the run-down motel.

"Tomorrow we'll start on the swimming pool," Jessie said.

"Oh, boy, the swimming pool," Benny echoed. "That's a good idea."

Once they were unpacked, they went back up the hill to have supper at Kay's. The dinner of roast lamb, mashed potatoes, and peas was delicious.

Aunt Jane passed the peas and said, "Kay, you have a lovely place here."

"Yes, it is," Kay agreed, "but it's so run-down that I've almost given up on it. In fact, I've had an offer from the Adventure Hotel chain. They are eager to buy the motel and I'm thinking of selling."

"Oh, no," Jessie said quickly, putting her fork down. "This place is too beautiful."

Kay gave her a small smile. "I know, Jessie, but it's too much for me. The only help I can afford is Rolf. Maybe I'll take the hotel money and rent an apartment."

"Kay!" Aunt Jane protested, "you can't do that. You wouldn't be happy in an apartment."

"We could help in fixing your place up, Kay," Violet said, eager as always to help someone in trouble.

Kay stood up. "I don't know," she said doubtfully, setting a cherry pie on the table.

"We're good fixer-uppers," Benny said.

"Yes, we are," Violet agreed. "A little paint would help and so would new bedspreads."

Kay sat down, cutting the pie into six pieces and placing a piece on each plate.

Jane helped pass the pie. "You know, Kay,

I think you should think about the children's offer. I can help, too. I can sew and I can redecorate."

Kay looked at the children's eager faces. "I don't know what to say. There's so much to be done."

"Make a list," Aunt Jane said practically, "and we'll take the work step by step. You'll see, it won't cost too much to do."

"The motel needs a coat of paint," Kay said thoughtfully. "And you kids could. . ." She stopped, hesitated, her eyes shining with hope.

"We could do whatever you want us to," Henry added.

Smiling, Kay leaned forward. "I'll give it a try! It's worth putting some more money into it."

Benny said, "We'll make your motel shine!"

But lying in bed that night, staring at the big Florida moon, Violet couldn't sleep. How could they possibly tackle all the work that the old motel needed!

CHAPTER 3

Millicent Fair

The second day the four Aldens scraped and scraped the green moss from the bottom of the pool. Fortunately, it wasn't a very large area. Kay was pleased at how clean the empty pool looked. So pleased that she promised to have it filled with water the next day, and to call the painters.

After cleaning the pool, the children biked to the small supermarket several blocks away. Grandfather had given them enough money to buy whatever they might need on their trip. Jessie took out the list which they'd all helped to write, and they went down the store aisles, filling the basket with green beans, peas, lettuce, tomatoes, fresh fruit, hamburger, chicken, ice cream, chocolate sauce, salad dressing, bread, butter, and milk. They also bought things for their breakfasts.

That evening, Jessie and Henry baked chicken for supper while Violet and Benny shelled peas and set the table.

After they had eaten fruit for dessert, they sat back and relaxed.

Benny asked, "Do you remember when we lived in the boxcar?"

"Do I!" Jessie exclaimed. "It was hard, but we had such good times, too."

Benny leaped up and ran to the cupboard. "Here's my pink cup that I found in the dump. It's all chipped and cracked, but I'll never throw it away!"

"Violet," Henry chimed in, taking his sister's hand, "if you hadn't become sick, Grandfather never would have found us."

"We ran away because we expected Grandfather to be a mean old man," Jessie said.

"And he was just the opposite," Henry said with a chuckle.

"We didn't have a mother or father," Benny said. "I'm glad Grandfather found us."

"Me, too," Henry replied. "I wonder how Grandfather is getting along without us."

"Oh, fine, I'm sure," Jessie said. "Mrs. McGregor will take good care of him!"

"And Watch will take care of himself," Violet said with a laugh. "Our dog is smart."

"I miss Watch," Jessie said.

Just then a loud "meow" was heard.

"It's Willie," Benny yelled, looking out the window. "He can take Watch's place while we're in Florida." He hurried to fling open the door.

Jessie found a string and played with Willie, but soon the cat went to the door. Henry let Willie out into the warm night and watched as the cat dashed up the hill to Kay's house.

Weary but happy, the Aldens undressed for bed.

* * *

The next morning, while they were eating a big breakfast of cereal, scrambled eggs, toast with grape jelly, and milk, someone tapped on the door.

Benny cracked open the door. A short plump woman peeked in. Her gray hair curled about her round face.

"Hello." She smiled sweetly. "I'm Millicent Fair. Call me Millicent," she said, stepping inside. "I want to say welcome."

"Hello," Jessie said pleasantly, "come in."

"Looks like I *am* in," Millicent said, hiding a giggle behind her hand. She bustled forward and dropped into a chair. "I heard you were visiting Kay." Her bright blue eyes darted from one Alden to the other. "How long are you staying?"

"We're not sure," Henry answered.

"I see you cleaned the swimming pool," she said happily.

"Yes," Jessie said. "We hope Rolf Jensen will fill it."

"It was a big job," Benny said, holding his palms outward. "See how red my hands are?"

"Why in the world are you doing all this?" Millicent Fair asked.

"We want to go swimming," Benny said.

"All this work." Millicent sighed. "Don't you know Kay plans to sell this place?"

"Kay's *not* going to sell," Jessie said, shaking her head hard.

"She's not?" Millicent said with surprise, leaning forward. "You mean she's staying?"

"We hope she will," Violet said softly. "And we're going to help all we can."

"With a little repair we'll make the motel look like new," Henry said. "Then Kay will stay for sure."

Millicent sank back in her chair. "I declare," she said. "And the Adventure Hotel chain made her such a splendid offer, too!"

"She told us," Jessie said, smiling. "But this is such a lovely spot, surrounded by cypress trees. Compared to the tall hotels, this motel has a cozy warm feeling."

"Wait until you see it when the painters are finished," Violet said.

"Painters?" Millicent's small mouth formed a big O.

"Yes, they'll be here today," Henry said. "Kay arranged for them last night."

"Soon this ugly brown paint will be painted over," Violet said.

"What color?" Millicent asked with interest.

"A glistening white," Violet responded.

"Won't the motel be beautiful set against the green grass and trees?" Jessie said.

Millicent blew out a breath of air, then she stood up. "Yes, it will be beautiful," she said. "I'm so glad!" Then she added, "I must go, but I'll see you soon."

When the two painters arrived, they began removing all the old paint. They appeared to be brothers, for they were both tall, though one was skinnier than the other. Each of them wore loose-fitting white overalls and white-billed caps from which a fringe of yellow hair stuck out from all angles.

At the end of the day they lined up six cans of white paint against the motel's outside wall.

"Won't the motel look nice and clean?"

Benny asked, his brown eyes twinkling with excitement.

"Yes, it will once the paint is on," Henry said.

Then Benny, his lower lip sticking out, said, "I'm hungry."

Jessie laughed. "I'm hungry, too, Benny."

They headed back to the motel, but this time they didn't hurry. They were too tired and their feet dragged.

That night they slept so deeply that they didn't hear a sound, not even the prowler outside their window.

In the morning, after breakfast, when Violet opened the door, her hand flew to her mouth. "Oh, no," she whispered.

"What is it?" Jessie asked, hurrying to her sister's side. She, too, stopped and stared. Benny and Henry joined them. They were speechless.

Someone had taken the paint. The painters hadn't arrived yet, so they hadn't done it. In the grass were circles where the six cans of paint had been. Not one can remained.

CHAPTER 4

Alligators and Swamp Birds

After one look at where the paint cans had been, Jessie hurried up the hill to get Kay.

Rolf, who was working at the house that morning, and Kay ran down to the motel, followed by Aunt Jane and Jessie.

Grimly, Kay surveyed the circles in the grass. "Six new cans of paint gone," she groaned, brushing back a strand of hair from her forehead. "What am I going to do?"

Aunt Jane stopped, too upset to move. Sympathetically, she touched Kay's hand.

"The painters won't be here until nine," Rolf said calmly, but he was also upset. He looked at Kay. "Do you want me to go into Lyndale and buy six more cans?"

Kay nodded. "I guess so." But she seemed uncertain.

As Rolf left, Kay, a worried look on her face, turned to the four children. "I don't understand. Why would anyone steal paint?"

Henry shrugged his shoulders. "We didn't hear a sound," he said.

"It's a good thing," Aunt Jane said. "Whoever did this wouldn't want to be caught. Who knows how they might have reacted."

Kay sighed and turned away. "Nothing can be done about the stolen paint." But suddenly she smiled. "Come up to the house, children. Aunt Jane and I were just about to have a cup of tea."

"Tea?" Benny asked.

Kay laughed. "For everyone else there's a pitcher of freshly squeezed orange juice."

"Oh, boy," Benny shouted. "I'm thirsty."

Violet laughed. "Then let's go up the hill."

The Aldens followed Kay and Aunt Jane.

As they climbed the slope Benny asked, "Will Rolf fill the pool today?"

"Maybe," Violet answered. "But if he does it will be after he's bought the paint in town."

In the dining room, Aunt Jane poured a glass of orange juice for each of the Aldens while Kay stared out the window. Every once in a while she took a sip of tea. "Why?" she murmured, glancing at Jane.

Aunt Jane sighed. "I wish we knew."

"Don't worry," Henry said to Kay. "We'll help you."

"Yes," Jessie said. "The stolen paint will soon be forgotten."

"I hope you're right," Kay said.

Aunt Jane changed the subject by reaching for a catalog from a large department store in Miami, and opened its pages to bedspreads. "Kay is going to order this style of bedspread for each unit. We decided last night."

"How lovely!" Jessie exclaimed, admiring the dust ruffle and quilted cover.

"Yes," Kay said. "Each unit will have a different color bedspread with matching drapes. The order should only take a day or two."

"What colors will you get?" Jessie asked, her voice rising with enthusiasm.

"Lots of colors," Kay replied, catching Jessie's good spirits. "Your unit will be lavender."

"Oh, good," Violet said. "My favorite color."

"I know," Kay said, the old sparkle appearing in her eyes.

"Does every unit have a little kitchen, Kay?" Benny asked.

"No," Kay replied. She stroked Willie. "Why do you ask, Benny?"

"I was thinking," Benny said. "Everybody likes to eat! You could serve breakfast in lunch boxes. Each box would be painted the color of the room."

"What an excellent idea," Kay said.

"And," Henry added, "each box could have a thermos of hot coffee."

"And muffins," Violet said.

"And orange juice," Jessie continued.

"Children, what marvelous ideas you've

given me," Kay said, her eyes sparkling.

"Then you'll definitely go ahead with painting the motel?" Aunt Jane questioned.

"Yes, I will!" Kay stood up so quickly that Willie leapt down with an annoyed *meow*. "I'm excited again about my Cypress Motel."

"So are we!" Henry said, a big grin creasing his face.

"You've been *so* helpful," Kay said. "Maybe when Rolf comes back he'll take you on the Everglades tour. He'll fill the pool after that and you can have a swim. Would you like to see the Everglades?"

"Yes!" Benny shouted. "I want to see an alligator."

"I'll bet you will, too," Henry said.

"Have fun," Kay said, opening the door. "I have work to do here but, Jane, wouldn't you like to go along?"

"I'd love to," Aunt Jane answered.

When Rolf pulled up in his red Jeep, he agreed a tour would be fine. A half hour later he drove them to the dock where his boat was tied. It was like a big rowboat with sides that had benches all around. Overhead was a canvas top striped like a circus tent.

Everyone scrambled aboard. Aunt Jane sat in front and the children sat in back. Jessie wore her camera around her neck, and Henry carried a pair of binoculars.

"I'm ready for a little relaxation myself," Rolf said as he steered the big boat out of the narrow channel and into open water. "Yesterday I put in a new sink at my own house and had a new refrigerator delivered."

"I'm glad this tour isn't a burden for you," Aunt Jane said.

Gulls dipped and soared above them. On either side of the boat were islands of trees. Long-legged blue herons walked along the shore. The birds moved carefully, as if they were on stilts.

"See that dark bird diving into the water?" Rolf asked, pointing to a bird just vanishing beneath the water.

"Yes, yes," Jessie said. "Now the bird is coming up. He's speared a fish with his sharp beak."

"The bird is an anhinga," Rolf said. "The other birds that you see in the distance with the wide bills are pelicans. Beyond the pelicans are pink birds called flamingos.

"Mangrove trees are edged along the islands," Rolf continued, indicating trees with thick trunks and leaves. "Mangroves are the only trees whose roots will grow in salt water."

Jessie peered through her camera lens, and when it was focused just right, she clicked the shutter. "I just shot a bald eagle circling his nest."

"He's a beauty," Henry said, his binoculars fastened to his eyes.

"That's a Southern bald eagle," Rolf explained. "It's fairly rare. See how large his nest is on top of that cypress tree?"

"Wow," Benny exclaimed. "I've never seen a nest as big as my bathtub!" He paused, looking in every direction. "But where are the alligators?"

"If we're lucky we'll see one," Rolf said.

"The Everglades are beautiful," Violet said, breathing in the warm August air.

"Yes," Rolf said, "and the many inlets are beautiful, too. But you have to know these narrow fingers of water or you could easily become lost."

Rolf knew everything, Violet thought, trailing her hand in the water. He probably knew everything about Kay's motel, too, as he came to work for her so often.

Suddenly a strange creature poked its head above water.

"Look! It's a dinosaur!" Benny shouted.

Rolf threw back his head and laughed. "No, Benny, that's a manatee or sea cow. It sort of looks like a walrus."

"Are manatees mean?" Benny asked, leaning forward to catch a closer look at the misshapen wrinkled head.

"No, they are clumsy and ugly, but they are gentle," Rolf said, putting on his sunglasses.

Suddenly, he asked, "Do you children have any idea who stole the paint?"

"No, we don't," Henry said, speaking for all of them.

"I wonder why Kay is working so hard. Do you think her motel is worth saving?" Rolf looked at the Alden children.

"I think it's charming," Jessie said. "It can be made beautiful."

"Yes, I agree," Henry stated positively.

"Sometimes I think she should sell," Rolf said. "It's too much for her." Abruptly he turned the boat around. "We've been out over three hours, time to get back."

"No alligator," Benny said with a disappointed scowl.

"Maybe we'll see one on the way back," Jessie said.

"No sooner said than done," Rolf said cheerfully. "Look over there!"

Violet shaded her eyes. "I see it! It's a huge alligator."

"Where?" Benny asked in an excited voice, squinting. "Where?"

"I see it, too," Henry said. "Look, Benny, do you see that gray log moving into the water?"

"Yes!" Benny said in a thrilled voice. "The log is a long alligator. It looks like its back is tree bark."

With a splash the alligator disappeared below the surface.

Benny smiled all the way back and was still smiling when Rolf pulled up to the dock. The tour had been a success for everyone. The whole mysterious world of the Everglades had opened up to them.

"Thanks, Rolf," Violet said, as she jumped nimbly from the boat to the dock.

"Yes, thanks," the others echoed, piling out of the boat. Aunt Jane was last. She grabbed Rolf's hand, and he pulled her firmly up to the dock. Smiling, she shook his hand. "I'll never forget our wonderful Everglades tour," she said.

"Good," Rolf said.

They sped along the winding road to Kay's.

"And now," Rolf said, pulling up before Kay's house, "I'll fill the swimming pool."

"Great," Henry said. "There's nothing I'd like better than a good swim to cool off." He jumped out of the Jeep and helped Benny down.

"I wonder how much the painters have done," Jessie said as she followed Henry, Violet, and Aunt Jane.

Standing before Kay's house, they looked down at the motel to see how much was finished. However, the painters weren't in sight.

Kay came around the house to meet them. She didn't look happy.

"What's wrong?" Rolf asked, striding toward her.

"The painters walked off the job shortly after you left." Upset, Kay bit her underlip.

"Why?" Rolf asked, concern showing in his dark eyes.

"No water," Kay answered crisply. "Someone cut off the water, and it can't be turned back on because there's a part missing. The painters refused to work in this heat without water." Wearily, she pushed back a strand of hair. "The plumber promised to come later today."

Violet glanced at Rolf. Again she thought how much Rolf knew about Kay's motel. Could Rolf have turned off the water? He did want her to sell it.

When they returned to the motel, Henry put out cheese and bread. Violet set out fruit

and cookies. Jessie set the table, and Benny poured the milk.

"Who could have shut off the water and stolen the paint?" Jessie wondered as they ate.

"Do you think it's the same person?" Violet asked.

"I do," Henry responded. "It's too much of a coincidence that two things should happen to stop work on Kay's motel."

"I hope it isn't Rolf," Violet said. "He's always so helpful." She took a deep breath. "But if you can put in a sink you need to know how to turn off water, don't you?"

"You sure do," Henry answered.

Oh, Violet thought, she shouldn't think such mean things about Rolf. It did seem, however, that someone was trying to stop Kay. She felt sorry for Kay, who was trying to save her motel. Now the pool couldn't be filled, and no painting had been done. What was going on?

CHAPTER 5

Oranges and More Oranges

The next morning the sun shone brightly, but there was a nice breeze. It was a good day to help Kay, Jessie thought. The plumber had brought the missing part the evening before, and now the water was turned on. A painter went by the window. All was going well.

Violet boiled water for poached eggs while Jessie broiled bacon. As Henry slid bread in the toaster and Benny poured the milk, there was a knock on the door.

Benny hopped down from his chair to answer.

Millicent Fair entered, proudly displaying a plate of muffins. She set them on the breakfast table. "Eat these banana-walnut muffins while they're still warm," she said with a smile, pulling up a chair before Henry could do it for her. Her sharp eyes darted from one to the other. "Where were you yesterday?" she asked. "I missed you."

"We went on Rolf's boat in the Everglades," Benny said. "And I saw an alligator!"

"Oh, my, Benny," Millicent Fair said, rolling her eyes toward the ceiling. "You had a big day. Did Kay stay home?"

"Yes," Jessie said, setting a glass of orange juice in front of Millicent.

"Did your Aunt Jane go on the tour?" Millicent questioned.

"Yes," Henry answered.

"Well, I had quite a day, too." She frowned. "There was not a drop of water," she said in a disapproving tone. "No water!"

"We know there was no water," Henry

said, wrinkling his forehead. "Someone deliberately shut it off!"

"You don't mean it," Millicent said, sinking back in her chair in surprise. After a brief pause, she leaned forward. "There are some queer things going on around here." With those words she drank her orange juice.

Violet gave Millicent a sharp look. Why had she been so eager to know where they'd been and what they were doing?

"Won't you have some breakfast?" Jessie asked politely.

Millicent jumped up, shaking her plump cheeks. "No, no, I must run. I have a hair appointment in Lyndale and the taxi will be coming any minute." She backed out, nodding and smiling.

After Millicent left, Henry said, "Millicent is certainly curious, isn't she?"

"I thought so, too," Violet said, eating the last piece of her bacon.

When they had finished eating and the dishes were washed, the Aldens chose four bikes from the bike shed for a ride. Waving to the painters, they pedaled past the swimming pool which Rolf had just filled that morning.

After circling the motel's grounds they headed out to the open road, riding beyond the store and to the edge of Lyndale.

When they returned, they placed the bikes in the bike shed.

"Let's go for a swim," Benny coaxed.

"First," Jessie said, "let's see if Kay needs our help."

"That's a good idea," Henry said.

The four children ran up the hill, eager to see what Kay needed.

When they arrived, Kay and Aunt Jane were sewing and talking.

"Hi, children," Kay said. "What are your plans for today?"

"We wanted to see if you needed anything done," Jessie said.

Kay smiled. "Aren't you sweet? I did call in the order for the bedspreads and drapes and they should arrive tomorrow," she said. "Then you could put them in each room, if you wanted to."

"Oh, yes we can do that," Violet said. "It

will completely change the look of the rooms."

"Thanks, everyone," Kay said. "The painters should finish soon. Yesterday I placed an ad about my motel in several northern papers. In a few months it will soon be time for my 'Snowbirds' to fly south."

"Snowbirds?" Violet asked quietly.

Kay smiled. "Yes, that's what we Floridians call tourists from the north who fly south for the winter. I'm hopeful that I'll soon be receiving reservations to fill my motel." Her eyes began to sparkle and once again she seemed full of hope. "In the meantime, how would you like to pick oranges?"

"Yes!" Benny shouted. "That will be fun."

"Good," Kay said. "If we're to serve orange juice every morning to tourists, I'll have to squeeze the juice and freeze it." She reached over and touched Benny's hand. "I don't know what I'd do without you. You're all as sweet and helpful as your Aunt Jane."

"Aw," Benny murmured. "It's nothing."

Jessie moved to the door. "The oranges are waiting for us."

They all laughed and followed her out to the backyard. They stood beneath the trees that were drooping with oranges ripe for the picking.

Leaning against the house was a ladder that Henry carried to the first tree. Jessie and Violet brought six bushel baskets from the same spot. They began to pull big oranges off the branches and drop them in the baskets.

The Aldens worked for an hour in the morning and came back in the afternoon. Catherine Wilson climbed the hill.

"Why are you picking all these oranges?" the attractive tall girl asked, glancing at the two full baskets.

"Kay intends to freeze juice for her winter tourists," Violet said.

"I hope her motel is better occupied than it is now," Catherine said.

"It will be!" Benny answered positively.

"I hope so," Catherine said, wiping her forehead with a handkerchief. "It's hot today," she said. "I just returned from the Seminole camp, and I think I need a swim.

Why don't you stop picking oranges and join me," she urged.

"We want to finish filling these baskets," Jessie said. "We will later."

"Please come," Catherine coaxed. "I don't want to swim alone."

"We'd like to," Henry said, placing several oranges in the basket, "but we'd better finish."

"The oranges will be there tomorrow," Catherine urged.

"Sorry," Violet said. "We'll join you later."

"Oh, all right," Catherine said in a disappointed voice. With a wave Catherine headed down the hill. How gracefully she moves, Jessie thought. She picked a big orange and tossed it down to Violet, still thinking about Catherine. Why did she want them to quit working? She had been so insistent.

When Kay came out, Jessie forgot her suspicions of Catherine. "Hi, Kay," she said, stepping down from the ladder.

"Why, you have six baskets brimming

with oranges!" Kay exclaimed. "How wonderful!" Thoughtfully, she tapped a finger on her chin. "Let's see, we'll put three baskets in the kitchen, and we'll leave the rest by the back door. I'll deal with those in the morning."

The children were pleased that they had helped Kay. "Now," Benny said, "you'll have lots and lots of orange juice."

Kay laughed. "You're right, Benny."

"Can we go for a swim now?" Benny asked, squinting up at Henry.

"You bet," Henry said.

They raced down the hill to change into their swimsuits.

When they got to the pool, Catherine had already left, but they had a splashing good swim.

After a supper of hamburgers, baked beans, and chocolate cake, they almost fell into bed. They were tired from a day of hard work and their long swim.

As they slept, a soft rain fell, but the children didn't awaken until Benny sat up in bed and complained, "Henry! Water is falling on my nose!"

Henry threw back his covers and hurried to Benny's bed. He pulled the bed away from the dripping ceiling. "It's the roof, Benny," he said. "I heard Rolf tell Kay that he'd repair it tomorrow." Without waking Jessie and Violet he tiptoed into the kitchen and found a pan to put under the leaky roof.

Benny and Henry went back to sleep and didn't open their eyes until the next morning.

Henry suggested a swim before breakfast.

"Hurrah!" Benny said. "I love to swim!" He pulled on his swim trunks and ran to the pool. But he didn't go in.

Instead he rushed back to the motel. "The oranges," he yelled. "Come, quick!"

Henry raced outside, followed by Jessie and Violet, who were also in swimsuits. When they reached the edge of the pool, they halted. They were too stunned to move another step.

There, before their eyes, three empty baskets and hundreds of oranges could be seen bobbing about on the clear water.

CHAPTER 6

Oranges, Oranges, Oranges

"The prowler strikes again!" Jessie exclaimed as she jumped into the pool and grabbed one orange after another, which she placed on the edge of the pool.

Benny, holding his nose, waded into the shallow end. He reached out and tried to catch an orange, but it rolled out of his hand.

Henry and Violet captured oranges, one by one, and set them on the grass above the pool.

"The oranges will soon dry in the sun," Violet said, jumping up and sitting on the

pool's edge. "I wish we could catch this prowler."

"That's the last one," Henry said, getting out. "We'd better tell Kay."

"Do we have to?" Violet asked, a note of regret in her voice.

Jessie jumped out, too, her wet skin glistening. "I agree with Henry," she said. "Kay needs to know what's going on at her own motel."

Violet breathed in deeply. "I suppose you're right," she said to Jessie, "but I'm afraid she'll become discouraged and sell to the Adventure Hotel chain."

Just then Catherine appeared. She was dressed in white pants and a yellow top, and she wore a red scarf around her head. Her smile was puzzled. "What are you doing with all these oranges?"

"Somebody threw them in the pool," Benny shouted, climbing up the ladder at the shallow end. "And after we picked oranges all day yesterday!"

Catherine's eyebrows rose. "That's strange," she said, sitting in a canvas chair.

Violet, her feet in the water, said, "It's *very* strange!"

Jessie vigorously dried down her brown hair. "We intend to find out who's doing all these things to Kay," she said.

Catherine was silent. Too silent, Violet thought.

"I'll meet you back at the motel for breakfast," Henry said. "I'll run up and tell Kay the bad news."

Catherine rose. "I must go, also."

"Are you visiting the Seminoles today, Catherine?" Violet asked.

"Yes, I've almost completed my paper so I only need to visit them two more times."

"What do you write about them?" Benny asked.

"I write about their habits and their camps," Catherine answered. "You know, Benny, the Seminoles who lived in Florida in the nineteenth century were forced to leave and re-settle in Oklahoma. Some, under their great chief, Osceola, tried to fight, but when Osceola was captured they hid out in the swamps and they still live there today."

"Wow," Benny said. "You're lucky, Catherine, to have Indian friends."

"I know, Benny," she said, glancing at her watch. "I'd better leave. Lacota will be waiting for me at the dock." She hesitated. "I'll be gone for a couple of days."

" 'Bye, Catherine," Violet said. "Thanks for taking the time to tell us about the Seminoles."

"I was glad to," Catherine said with a sweet smile.

Violet watched Catherine's car leave. Catherine was such a lovely girl. She certainly couldn't be guilty of doing anything bad.

"Do you think Catherine would introduce me to Lacota?" Benny asked.

Violet shook her head. "I doubt it, Benny. The Native Americans are friends with Catherine, but they might not like a stranger coming into their homes."

Disappointed, Benny said only one word. "Oh."

"Are you hungry?" Violet asked, standing.

"Breakfast!" Benny said. "I almost forgot."

"Come on, then, let's give Jessie a hand." Violet and Benny dashed back to their unit.

When they arrived, they found Jessie mixing pancake batter, and Henry, who had returned from Kay's, broiling sausages.

"Just in time to eat," Henry said, dishing up the sausages. "Sit down, Benny."

Violet set the syrup and butter on the table and poured the milk while Jessie placed a steaming stack of pancakes before Benny.

"How did Kay take the news about the oranges?" Violet asked.

Henry helped himself to several sausages and passed them to Jessie. "Kay wasn't happy about it, but she's determined to go ahead with redoing the motel."

"Good," Violet said, breathing a sigh of relief.

"Aunt Jane is going into Lyndale this morning with Kay. They're stopping at the bank where Kay plans to ask for a loan," Henry added.

"I hope she gets it," Jessie said.

"I hope so, too," Henry replied. "After

they go to the bank, Aunt Jane and Kay are staying in town for shopping and lunch."

"Good for them," Violet said.

"W-e-ll," Jessie said, drawing out the word and smiling slyly. "Kay did say the bed-spreads and drapes will arrive today and if we wanted to — "

"If we wanted to!" Violet said eagerly. "Of course we want to!"

"Want to what?" Benny said, licking his fork for the last drop of syrup.

Violet's brown eyes twinkled. "Want to unpack the bedspread and drapes and fix up each room."

"Yes!" Benny said. "We'll have a big sur-prise for Aunt Jane and Kay."

"We sure will," Henry said with a chuckle. "Kay said we all needed a break and that we should loaf today and go biking and swim-ming."

"We can do that and put on the spreads, too," Jessie said, clearing her plate and glass. She smiled at Benny.

CHAPTER 7

Glittering Yellow Eyes

The Aldens made up the beds with the brightly flowered bedspreads. Then they unpacked the matching drapes and in the afternoon, using the master key that Kay had given Jessie, hung them in Millicent's and Catherine's units. Neither was home so it was easy to work in their rooms.

While stripping off the pillows in Catherine's room, Jessie brushed her arm against a book on the end table. The book clattered to the floor and a map fell out. She glanced at the map, noticing it was of the area. She was about to slip it back in the pages, when she glimpsed a red marking. "Look, Henry," she said in a puzzled tone. "This map has Kay's motel circled in red." She stopped. "And Adventure Hotel is circled, too!"

"That *is* strange," he said. "But put it back. It probably doesn't mean anything."

Jessie wasn't as sure as Henry that it didn't mean anything.

"Won't Catherine and Millicent be surprised when they return?" Violet asked.

Jessie nodded, replacing the map and saying nothing.

After lunch, they decorated their own rooms. Henry stood on a ladder, pulling the lovely lavender drape across the rod, while Jessie and Violet made the beds.

Violet stood back and gazed at her bed. "Isn't it beautiful?" she asked, admiringly.

"Won't Kay be pleased when she returns?" Jessie said.

"Can we go for a swim now?" Benny asked. "I'm hot."

"Even in this air conditioning?" Violet asked.

"Yes." A smile lit Benny's round face. "I could go swimming in the winter."

"I'm ready for a swim, too," Jessie said.

So once again they pulled on their swimsuits and raced to the pool.

Henry made a clean dive into the clear water. Jessie stood on the diving board and dived into the water. Violet waded in with Benny at the shallow end.

Henry swam under the water and came up underneath Benny, who screamed with delight when he was lifted on Henry's shoulders. Jessie and Violet swam easily around their brothers.

The Aldens were swimming and laughing so hard that they didn't hear Aunt Jane and Kay arrive until the two women were at the edge of the pool.

Kay smiled. "You darlings! Jane I went to your room and peeked in, and what a wonderful surprise! We saw the whole motel changed with new spreads and drapes."

Aunt Jane smiled warmly at each child. "We couldn't resist checking out the other units, too, and it was hard to believe our eyes! What a difference to see each room with a style and color of its own." She held out her hand, pulling Violet out of the water. "You must have been working ever since we left."

Kay looked around. The painters had finished, except for the trim and the bike shed, and the white motel gleamed in the sun. Kay gave a contented sigh. "I almost received my bank loan. I'll know tomorrow morning after the bank inspector comes to look over the motel. If he likes what he sees, I'll get the money."

"He'll like the motel!" Benny said in a loud voice. "How couldn't he not like it?"

Kay laughed and leaned over, giving him a hug.

"Have any reservations come in yet?" Henry questioned.

A brief frown flickered across Kay's face. "Not yet. I should be receiving the reservations from my regular Snowbirds and also a few from my newspaper ads."

Aunt Jane removed her straw hat and brushed back a loose strand of hair. "I'd like an iced tea, wouldn't you, Kay?"

"Yes," Kay responded. "That sounds like an excellent idea. Won't you join us, children?"

They looked at one another and shook their heads. "No, Kay," Jessie said, "but thank you. We want to go for a bike ride and then — "

"And then," Benny piped up, "we'll eat!"

Henry's eyes sparkled. "Yes, we have a special supper planned."

Benny rubbed his stomach. "Chicken and mashed potatoes."

"And broccoli," Violet said.

"And strawberry Jell-O," Jessie added. "Topped off with ice cream and cookies."

"Ummm," Kay said, "that does sound good."

"Boy, I can't wait to eat. I'm going to have two helpings of everything!" Benny said.

And that night for supper that's exactly what he did.

They all went to bed with full stomachs and a happy feeling that they had had such a successful day.

As she was drifting off to sleep, Violet

turned in bed and was astonished to see a shadow outlined in her window. Then it disappeared. Her heart pounded and she jumped out of bed. "Jessie! Henry! Someone just went by my window!"

Without a second's delay, Henry found his flashlight and flung open the door.

Sleepily, Benny joined them. "What's wrong?" he said with a wide yawn.

"Shhh," Violet cautioned. "Someone's out there."

Benny tiptoed outside behind Henry.

Henry shone the flashlight into the trees, but nothing stirred.

Suddenly Jessie's hand flew to her mouth, stifling a scream. "H-he's on top of the motel," she stammered.

Henry shot the beam up on the roof. He stiffened with fear.

The white beam of light caught two yellow eyes.

Frightened, they stared at the glittering yellow eyes that moved closer and closer.

CHAPTER 8

The Lights Go Out

The four Aldens watched the yellow eyes, too scared to move. Closer and closer they came.

All at once Benny began to laugh. "It's Willie," he hooted gleefully.

Henry held the flashlight steady, and sure enough, as the cat crept to the edge of the roof, they could see Willie's furry form.

With a meow, Willie leapt to a tree limb and scampered away up to Kay's house.

"Whew!" Henry said. "Am I glad the prowler turned out to be Willie!"

"But I saw a *person* in my window," Violet protested.

"You must be mistaken," Jessie said quietly as she opened the door of their motel. "You may have imagined a shadow, Violet, but it was only a cat."

"No," Violet mumured. "I know it was a person!"

But either they didn't hear Violet's words or they didn't believe her. Everyone went to bed, relieved it had been only Willie.

With a sigh, Violet snuggled beneath the covers and tried to sleep. It was a long time, however, before she dreamed of shadows and faces at the window.

In the morning after a breakfast of orange juice, Shredded Wheat with sliced bananas, and toast, they sat awhile and discussed Kay's motel.

"You know," Jessie said, resting her folded hands on the table, "Millicent is always buzzing in and out and asking questions."

"I know," Violet answered. "What do you suppose she's up to?"

"Nothing!" Benny protested. "Millicent brings us good things to eat."

"You're right, Benny," Jessie agreed. "I'm a little suspicious of Catherine. Remember how she wanted us to stop picking oranges?"

"She asks questions, too," Violet responded.

"I don't know," Henry said, his dark eyes serious. "It could be Rolf. Did you hear him say he thinks Kay should sell."

"That's right," Jessie said.

"I think he likes Kay," Benny said.

"I agree, Benny," Violet said. "I've seen Rolf's eyes light up when he looks at her."

"Millicent isn't the one," Benny said, nodding his head. "And Catherine isn't either. Rolf couldn't be. They're all too nice."

"What if it's just a prowler?" Jessie asked. "Maybe it's no one we know."

Henry shook his head doubtfully. "Someone's after Kay and her motel, and I'll bet it's someone we know."

"Enough guessing," Jessie said, standing. "Let's help Kay get the motel ready for the bank inspector."

"Yes," Violet agreed. "Let's go up to Kay's house."

The Aldens, wearing jeans, T-shirts, and sneakers, went outside. They were upset at how dark and gloomy the day had become. Thunder rumbled in the distance.

"Isn't it too bad the sun isn't shining?" Violet said.

Jessie nodded. "Yes. The motel is so much prettier in the bright sunshine."

Violet said, "Let's turn on the lamps in each unit."

"Good idea, Violet," Jessie said. "I still have the key Kay gave us when the bedspreads arrived."

Benny looked up at the sky. "Look how dark it is, and how fast the clouds are flying!"

"Yes, I'm afraid it's going to pour any minute," Henry said.

"No matter," Jessie said, smiling. "We'll make each motel room bright and cheery with lots of light."

They began at Catherine's unit since she wasn't home. Benny flipped on the switch. Frowning, he muttered, "Where's the light?"

Henry chuckled. "Did you see if the cord is plugged into the outlet?"

Benny followed the cord to the outlet, and wiggled it back and forth. "It's plugged in!" he said. "I tested it!"

"Hmmmm," Jessie said. "Let's see if the bulb is screwed tightly into the socket." She twisted the bulb and it was tight.

Violet tried the bathroom light. Nothing!

Henry said in a worried voice, "Let's see if the lights are off in the other units."

Sure enough, there were no lights.

Millicent Fair came out of her unit. "My lights won't work," she complained. "I'm not staying here! I've called a cab, and I'm going to the Adventure Hotel for breakfast!"

"Millicent!" Benny said. "Somebody fixed the lights so they wouldn't light."

Millicent stared with wide eyes at Benny. "Why, that's terrible," she said, grabbing her purse. "You know what I think?" She leaned forward and whispered, "I think this place is jinxed!"

Soon a yellow taxi pulled up to Millicent's unit and she hurried in. She shut the door

with a bang, not once looking back at the children.

Jessie's forehead wrinkled. "What if new tourists who rent Kay's units find out what's been happening?"

Violet bit her lip. "They won't stay here."

"It's jinxed!" Benny yelled. "Millicent said so."

"No, Benny," Henry said firmly. "The motel is *not* jinxed! That's why we've got to get to the bottom of who's doing these things!"

Just then a car door slammed. Violet glanced toward Kay's house. A blue car with the words BANK OF LYNDALE was parked in front.

"The inspector is here," Violet said in a low sad voice. "He won't be able to see how pretty the motel really is."

"If only the sun could have shone like yesterday," Jessie said. "The place looks lovely in the sun."

"Here he comes," Henry warned.

Kay and the inspector walked down the hill. Kay gestured with her hands as she eagerly talked to the tall skinny man at her side. The bank inspector, dressed in a black suit and carrying a black umbrella, pressed his lips together in a thin line.

"Oh, oh," Benny said. "He won't like it 'cause it looks like he doesn't like anything. Besides, it's so dark he can't see the motel very well!"

"I think he'll be able to see enough," Jessie said encouragingly. But in her heart she wondered. They could have made the motel look so cozy and bright in the lamplight. Who turned off the lights? She was certain it was no accident.

Lightning zigzagged across the black sky, and a crack of thunder boomed. The Aldens hurried inside where they sat huddled around a table, waiting for the inspector.

Jessie rose and found two candles, then she quietly sat down again. Poor Kay, she thought. She has the worst luck in the world. If she didn't get the loan, the roof wouldn't be repaired, and all the other things she wanted to fix would go undone. She would have to sell.

CHAPTER 9

Mr. Smiley

In the flickering candlelight the Aldens sat quietly at the table. The bank inspector would be there any minute. The thunder rumbled and the lightning flashed.

It wasn't long before the pinch-faced man and Kay entered their room. Kay introduced them to Mr. Smiley. But he didn't look very smiley, Benny thought. He looked more scowly. Mr. Smiley barely nodded as he snooped around the motel. He sniffed as he poked at a bed with his umbrella.

Kay winked at the children as Mr. Smiley

walked into the kitchen. Henry gave Kay a thumbs-up sign. They heard the faucet run and the gas stove turn on.

Mr. Smiley came into the room and said, "I've seen enough, Mrs. Kingsley, to make an honest assessment." Glancing at the children, he again nodded coldly. Holding the door open for Kay, Mr. Smiley followed her out of the room.

Jessie breathed a sigh of relief. "Whew," she said. "I'm glad that's over!"

"Do you think Kay will get the loan?" Violet asked quietly.

"He looked too fussy to me," Benny said, lifting his nose in the air, pretending to be Mr. Smiley.

Suddenly, the rain came down in torrents. Henry rushed for a pot to place under the leak above where Benny's bed used to be.

Jessie took down a game from the closet shelf. "This is a good day to play Monopoly," she said.

"Yes, it is," agreed Violet. "Isn't it nice that Kay has all kinds of games and cards for tourists to check out?"

They played Monopoly for over an hour.

"The rain has stopped," Jessie said.

Henry opened the door and drops of water fell from the roof. The dark sky, however, had changed to a light gray, and in the east was a rosy-pink streak, which meant the sun might shine after all.

"Let's go for a bike ride," Benny said eagerly, pushing the board away. "Violet won."

"Okay, Benny," Violet answered. "We can stop at the store and buy bread."

They all helped to put the game back neatly.

Henry went outside and glanced up at Kay's house. Mr. Smiley's car was gone. Coming back in, he said, "Let's swing around by Kay's and see if she was given the bank loan."

"Oh, yes," Jessie said, holding up two crossed fingers for luck. "I hope."

"And let's call Grandfather," Benny said.

"Oh, good, Benny," Violet said. "We will."

Wheeling out the bikes from the nearby

shed, they pedaled single file up the narrow path to Kay's house.

Kay and Aunt Jane were picking roses that grew near the house. The pink blossoms glistened with raindrops.

Aunt Jane turned and smiled. "Hi, children. Did you sleep well last night?"

"After Willie jumped off the roof," Henry said, straddling his bike, "we were fine."

Kay laughed. "My cat likes to roam at night."

"Does he ever!" Jessie said. "Willie's yellow eyes gave us quite a scare."

"We were wondering what Mr. Smiley had to say," Violet asked shyly.

Kay said in a deep voice like Mr. Smiley's, " 'After much thought, I *will* recommend that you be granted a loan.' "

"Hurrah!" Benny yelled. Jessie laughed in delight at Kay's imitation.

Now Kay's voice was lighthearted. "I've already phoned Rolf, and he's in Lyndale right now buying shingles to patch the roof. He's also bringing fuses. He thinks someone stole the fuses from the fuse box and that's what made the lights go out."

"Good!" Benny said. "Now we can see, but who did it?"

"I wish we knew," Kay said. "Too many things are happening!"

"Whoever it is, the person will be caught," Violet said, trying to reassure Kay.

"When Rolf fixes the roof, no more rain will drip on my face," Benny said, his face brightening.

Kay chuckled. "That's right, Benny. No more leaks in the roof."

"May we call Grandfather?" Jessie asked.

"Please," Kay answered, gesturing to the phone on the desk.

Jessie dialed the number and told Grandfather Alden what a good time they were having. Violet said hello and didn't mention any of the mysterious goings on, for fear that he'd worry. Benny eagerly told him about the orange trees and the swimming pool.

After each Alden had talked to Mr. Alden, Henry went over to Kay. "Could we bring you anything?" he offered. "We're biking to the store."

Kay glanced at Jane, who shook her head. "I don't think we need a thing, but thanks," Kay said.

Cheerfully waving good-bye, the children biked down the muddy lane.

At the store, Jessie bought a loaf of bread. That errand over, they biked to the edge of Lyndale and back.

When they returned, Kay called to them, "Rolf is back with the shingles and has already replaced the missing fuses. He needs a little help with the shingles."

Benny shouted. "I'll help."

"And so will I," Henry volunteered.

"Wonderful," Kay said. "I think he just needs someone to hand him the shingles."

"What can we do?" Violet asked.

Kay smiled. "See all these geraniums? They need potting. I have window boxes stored in the bike shed."

"Oh, what fun," Jessie said. "We'll plant the flowers in the boxes and put them on the windowsills of each motel unit."

"Right," Kay said.

"Won't the red flowers be pretty against

the white motel?" Violet said.

"I thought so," Kay said. "If you'll do that, Jane and I have a sewing project. You know the small round table by each bed. We're going to make tablecloths to cover each one in all the units."

"Aunt Jane is a beautiful seamstress," Violet said.

Kay chuckled. "I know. She's already hemmed a skirt for me."

Rolf climbed the hill. "Hi, kids," he called. "It's good to see the sun again, isn't it?"

"Yes," Benny said, looking up at the big man. "Henry and I will help you with the shingles!"

"Then let's get started," Rolf said. "My Jeep is parked below, filled with shingles. Come on, kids." He hoisted Benny up on his shoulders.

"I'm a roofer today," Rolf said with a grin, setting Benny on the ground. Rolf wore a cap, jeans, and a navy shirt and looked quite handsome. "Do you want to bring me a bundle of shingles from the Jeep, Henry, while I get the ladder?"

"Sure thing," Henry said, eager to start.

The girls hauled out eight window boxes and filled them with potting soil from the bags that were lined up against the shed. Then they took the crimson geraniums and planted the first window box.

Rolf placed the ladder against the motel.

Benny shaded his eyes as Rolf climbed halfway up the ladder. "Will you stop the rain from dripping in my eyes?"

"I'm going to patch that very spot," Rolf promised.

Shingles were stacked high in the back of the jeep.

Henry reached in for a stack but quickly pulled his hand away. Puzzled, he stared at his sticky fingers.

Benny, coming up behind Henry, also tried to lift a shingle, but it was stuck fast.

"Ugh!" Benny said, wiping a thick black substance on the grass. "It won't come off," he wailed. "What is it, Henry?"

"I think it's tar," Henry said.

The shingles were ruined. Someone had poured tar all over them.

CHAPTER 10

Running Water

"Rolf!" Henry shouted. "Look at this!"

Rolf stepped off the ladder and walked over to Henry. "What is it?" Then he saw the black tar oozing over the new shingles. "For Pete's sake," he muttered, planting his hands on his hips and shaking his head "Who did this?"

"I wish I knew." Henry looked at Rolf with a stricken expression. Rolf seemed very calm. To Henry, Rolf didn't seem upset, nearly enough.

Benny's chin stuck out and he said in a loud voice. "I wish we could find this mean person!" He shook his fist in the air. "I'd like to give him a punch!"

Henry's hand dropped on Benny's shoulder. "I know, Benny. But don't worry, we'll find out who's behind this!"

"I'll just have to haul the whole mess to the dump," said Rolf.

Violet and Jessie hurried over to see what all the fuss was about. Jessie stared at the ruined shingles. "Well, this tops it," she said angrily. "I think Kay should hire a detective!"

Thoughtfully, Rolf smoothed his mustache. "Let's not be too hasty about hiring a detective. We'll talk to Kay first."

Henry gave Rolf a sideways glance. Was Rolf *afraid* of a detective? He was always at the scene of trouble, and he knew Kay's motel like his own place. He was able to replace the fuses in a flash, knowing just which ones controlled which units.

"Come on, Henry and Benny. Let's go up to Kay's," Rolf said.

All at once Millicent and Catherine appeared.

"We heard the commotion," Catherine said, "and came out to take a look. Who spoiled the shingles?"

Jessie shrugged. "The same person who's upset Kay's plans for the motel." Jessie was surprised to see Catherine. She thought she was with the Seminoles. You never knew where Catherine was. When you believed she was out in the Everglades, she was there at the motel. Hastily Jessie returned to her planting, afraid Catherine might see the doubt in her face.

"Oh, dear, oh, dear," Millicent said, placing a palm against her round cheek. "I'm astonished Kay would stay here after this! She's had one problem after another."

"Kay is a fighter," Violet said quietly. "Maybe she'll hire a detective to find out who's doing these things."

Millicent's eyes grew wide. "Oh, I wouldn't think that would be necessary," she said. "Maybe the tar spill was an accident."

Jessie stopped patting dirt around a red

geranium to stare at Millicent. Was she serious? What a weird thing to say. Perhaps Millicent was the guilty one. Jessie hid a smile. It was hard to imagine that Millicent knew how to turn off the water and lights.

"I just don't know," Millicent said. "I've just retired and want a little relaxation and" — she waved a plump hand in the air — "all these things happen. I said it before and I'll say it again — Kay's motel is jinxed."

Jessie stood up and said as calmly as possible, "I don't think so, Millicent. Whoever the prowler is, he's as much alive as you and I."

"Well," Millicent announced, "I'm only staying until the end of the week. All this hullabaloo is hard on my nerves!"

"Meow," went Willie, rubbing against Millicent's ankle.

"Heavens! The cat!" squealed Millicent. All at once she sneezed — three tiny sneezes in a row. "Why, oh, why, does that beast come near me!"

Catherine gathered Willie in her arms.

"Cats seem to know when someone doesn't like them," she said. "Willie just wants to make friends with you."

Millicent threw up her hands in despair. "I'm going inside before I break out." Rapidly she breathed in and out. "My allergy, you know." And off she went as fast as her short legs could carry her, sneezing all the way.

As soon as Millicent was gone, Willie leapt out of Catherine's arms and padded over to a tree where he clawed the bark.

Catherine said, "Time is running out for me. On Monday I return to the university." Smiling, she said, "My money supply is running out, too. Renting a car and staying in a motel are expensive." She paused. "Although Kay's motel is much more reasonable than the big hotels."

"We'll be sorry to see you go," Violet said sincerely. "We just get acquainted and then we're separated."

Jessie nodded in agreement. "Your work with the Seminoles is fascinating, Catherine. We'd like to hear more."

"Maybe tomorrow," Catherine replied. "Today I'm hitting the books."

"Don't work too hard," Violet said.

"And that goes for you, too," Catherine said as she turned and went into her unit.

Jessie couldn't help thinking that if Catherine were the guilty one, she'd be gone in a few days.

Rolf, Henry, and Benny came down the hill from Kay's. Benny ran ahead and bent down to see what the girls were planting in the window boxes.

"Kay's not going to hire a detective," Henry said, standing over the kneeling girls. He leaned over and handed Violet a geranium plant. "Kay thinks we can find the person doing all this ourselves."

"I hope she's right," Violet said doubtfully.

"Besides," Benny added, "Kay says a detective would cost too much."

"She's right there," Rolf said. "A detective would be expensive, and Kay has plenty of bills to pay already. The new shingles alone will cost enough."

Jessie stood up. "Kay must be wondering if she should invest any more money in her motel. I know I'd begin to think about it."

Rolf walked toward his Jeep.

"Are you leaving now?" Violet asked.

"Yes," Henry said, moving to Rolf's side. "We're going to the dump and get rid of the shingles, and then drive to Lyndale to buy more."

"Coming, Benny?" Rolf called, climbing in the driver's seat.

Benny dashed forward, got into the Jeep, and slid toward the middle while Henry got in on the other side.

The girls watched the Jeep roar down the lane.

"I have a feeling," Violet said. "that the prowler has more plans for Kay's motel."

Jessie laughed. "Is that just a feeling or do you know something I don't?"

Violet smiled, giving a slight shrug. "I guess it's a feeling 'cause I don't know anything for certain."

"Well, maybe we'll find out soon," Jessie said lightly.

After using up the bags of potting soil, the girls had filled eight window boxes. The red blooms, small now, would grow quickly.

One by one Jessie and Violet carried the window boxes and set them on the wide window ledge of each unit.

Jessie stepped back to admire the flowers. "For every wrong thing, there's a right one," she said, wiping her smudged cheek.

Violet laughed. "You're right. Look how the motel has changed since our arrival."

They had one more task. Carefully dragging the water hose out of the bike shed, they watered each window box.

Pleased with their day's work, the girls showered and dressed in fresh shorts and T-shirts and went to the pool for an hour.

"It seems like we're always at the pool," Violet said.

Jessie laughed. "That's what you do when you stay at a motel to relax."

When the boys arrived, they were hot and tired. "Rolf bought new shingles," Henry said. "He was right. The shingles were pretty expensive."

"It's a good thing Kay isn't doing the whole roof," Violet commented.

"I know," Jessie said. "I'm glad she got the loan, just in case there are any more unpleasant surprises. After seeing Mr. Smiley, I didn't think he'd give her the money."

Henry chuckled. "I didn't either, Jessie. I'll never forget his sour face."

"When is supper?" Benny asked.

"Six-thirty," answered Violet. "First, though, will you set the table?"

"Sure, I will," Benny said, and he promptly went to the shelves to get the dishes.

After a supper of broiled fish, string beans, and baked potatoes, the Aldens played another lively game of Monopoly. They finished the day by eating a bowl of ice cream that dripped with butterscotch sauce.

Getting ready for bed, Jessie felt uneasy. What nonsense, she thought. Violet was the one who had the feeling that something bad would happen.

But for two days nothing happened. One

day it was sunny, so the Aldens biked, swam, and went into Lyndale, while the next day was rainy so they played games, visited with Aunt Jane and Kay, and played with Willie.

That night, however, shortly after midnight, Jessie awoke to the sound of running water. Something's wrong, she thought, and her heart began to pound.

Quickly, she threw back her covers and stepped out of bed.

To her horror her feet touched cold water.

Drawing her legs back, she called hoarsely, "Violet! Violet, wake up!"

"Hmmmm?" Violet said drowsily. She sat up, rubbing her eyes. "What is it, Jessie?"

"Water!" Jessie said in an alarmed voice. "Water is everywhere!"

Fully awake, Violet reached over and turned on the bedside lamp. Sure enough, water covered the floor.

"Where's the water coming from?" Violet asked urgently.

"I don't know," Jessie replied, a prickle of fear running down her spine.

CHAPTER 11

The Suspects

Henry rushed out of his bedroom, followed by Benny. "What's all the commotion?" Henry asked.

"Don't take another step," Violet warned.

Henry glanced down and saw the water edging toward him.

Curious, Benny ran forward and stopped abruptly when he found himself standing in water. He lifted one bare foot, then the other. "Why is there water on the floor?"

"We're not sure," Jessie said as calmly as she could.

Henry rolled up his pajama bottoms and raced to the front door where the sound of gushing water was loudest.

Jessie hurried to Henry's side, followed by Violet. Benny was last, splashing through the water.

"The garden hose!" Jessie exclaimed. "The nozzle's stuck in the window box and all our poor geraniums plants are drowned!"

The hose, pouring forth water, had over-flowed from the window box through the open window, and into their room.

Without wasting a minute, Jessie raced to the outside faucet and turned it off.

Water ran along the outside wall, flooding the soil along the motel's foundation. "This could have been serious," Henry said.

Violet hurried out and grabbed a mop from the supply closet. She swished the mop back and forth on the floor and then wrung it out in the sink. Henry grasped a broom and swept water outside.

Jessie, using rags, soaked up water along the baseboards.

Benny, though, hadn't moved. He conti-

ued to stare at the wet floors. "Millicent was right," he said. "The motel is jinxed!"

Jessie rose and said, "No, Benny. A real person is causing the damage."

A frown crossed Henry's face as he paused in his sweeping. "If the water kept running, it could have seeped through the wall cracks into the next unit."

Jessie's brown eyes flashed. "Of everything that has happened, this is the worst!"

"I knew something would happen," Violet murmured.

"Let's go to bed," Jessie said. "We've cleaned up the water."

"I won't sleep!" Benny said.

Henry smiled and put his hand on Benny's shoulder. "Oh, I think you will."

But that night none of the Aldens slept well. Henry's thoughts were on the prowler — was he still hanging around? Jessie thought of danger — would whoever was doing these awful things turn violent? Violet wondered what the prowler would do next. And Benny kept thinking he saw shadows and heard mysterious noises.

* * *

In the morning, Jessie climbed the hill to inform Kay of the deliberate attempt to flood her motel.

At first Kay didn't reply, but then her eyes took on a steely look. "I can't believe anything else is going to go wrong, but I'll call Officer Miller just the same. He'll patrol the place at night."

Aunt Jane, who had been standing in the doorway in her robe, now moved to Jessie's side. "You poor children," she said. "You must have been scared to death. Shall we call Grandfather and go home?"

"We weren't afraid," Jessie said boldly. She didn't want to alarm her aunt. But the image of Benny's face when he'd said the motel was jinxed stuck in her mind.

Kay chatted on, trying to sound unconcerned, though she looked *very* concerned. "Rolf was over for dinner last night and stayed quite late. He promised to come over today and check on the painters. It's their last day to finish some retouching. He also promised to shingle parts of the roof."

Jessie became instantly alert. The water had been turned on about midnight, when she'd been awakened. "What time did Rolf leave?" she asked in a casual tone.

"Oh," Kay said, "I guess it was midnight."

So, Jessie thought, was Rolf the guilty one after all? Had he been prowling about outside their motel? But why? He seemed to really like Kay.

"Is something wrong?" Aunt Jane questioned.

"What?" Jessie said weakly. "Oh, no, no." She backed up, a nervous feeling in her stomach. She liked Rolf. "I have to go," she said lamely, trying to smile. "Or they won't leave me a bite of breakfast."

Slowly Jessie walked down the hill. How she hated to tell her sister and brothers about her suspicions. But the sooner they knew and Kay knew, the sooner these awful things would stop. She wondered if Rolf would be sent to jail.

Entering the motel, Jessie brushed back her hair. Benny was the first to greet her. "Pancakes, Jessie," he said, smiling. "We've been waiting for you to get back."

"We've kept breakfast hot," Violet said.

Sitting down, Jessie dully told them about Rolf. "And," she ended, "midnight was when the running water woke me up."

"I can't believe that Rolf is the one. He always wants to help." Henry hesitated. "Yet he did haul the shingles in his Jeep. It would have been easy to pour tar on them."

"But there's no proof," Violet said, a slight frown creasing her forehead. "We must be certain."

She passed the bacon to Jessie, but Jessie shook her head. "I can't eat," she said miserably. Rolf had been everyone's friend.

Benny drank his orange juice and said, "Rolf isn't the mean one. I rode piggyback on his shoulders downhill."

"I don't think we should overlook Catherine," Violet said. "As much as we all like her, Catherine was here all day and night yesterday."

"That's right," Jessie said thoughtfully.

"I don't know," Henry said. "She's so sweet."

"And pretty!" Benny added.

"We can't blame anyone," Violet said practically. "We have no proof."

"Maybe it's Millicent," Benny said. "She's a spy who learns a lot about Kay's motel by giving us things to eat."

"Millicent?" Henry asked with a chuckle. "She's just a nice little old lady."

Quietly they sat at the table, each thinking about the suspects.

They spent the afternoon at the pool and that night they had one of Benny's favorite suppers, hamburgers, tomatoes, baked potatoes, and hot fudge sundaes.

They slept well.

In the morning, as they were eating their cereal with sliced bananas, Millicent called, "Yoo-hoo, may I come in?"

Henry glanced at Jessie. "Here's Millicent again," he whispered, smiling. "I wonder what she has today."

Benny jumped off his chair and ran to the door.

Millicent hurried in. "I woke up at six so

I baked chocolate chip cookies this morning."

Benny rolled his eyes at Violet.

Millicent smiled. As she set the plate on the table, she stumbled. Her large handbag dropped to the floor, and the contents spilled out.

"Dear, dear," she said, stooping down and trying to gather up everything. Violet, however, was faster. She scooped up several letters, and as she handed them to Millicent, she caught a glimpse of the addresses. They read: MS. KAY KINGSLEY CYPRESS MOTEL LYNSDALE, FLORIDA.

Millicent snatched the letters from a shocked Violet. "I-I must hurry along." She nodded quickly in a nervous way. "Enjoy the cookies, children."

As soon as the door shut, Violet said in a shaky voice, "Millicent Fair had Kay's mail. I saw the envelopes!"

The children stopped eating to stare at Violet.

Finding his voice, Henry asked Violet, "Do you think those letters could have been reservations for the motel?"

Violet nodded, answering, "I saw lots of letters and they all had Kay's name on them."

"If that's true, then it's no wonder Kay hasn't received reservations from her Snowbirds," Jessie said.

"Did Millicent steal letters from Kay's mailbox?" Benny asked, his voice rising in surprise.

"Yes," Violet stated. "That must be exactly what she's been doing."

"Didn't I tell you?" Benny asked smugly. "I knew Millicent was a spy with her sweets."

"It would be easy to sneak the letters out of the mailbox," Henry said thoughtfully. "It's on the edge of the road and open to anyone."

Jessie quickly placed her plate and glass in the sink. "I'm sure Millicent noticed Violet's reaction to the letters. My guess is that she's packing right now."

Benny was already at the door. "Aren't we going to tell Kay?"

They looked up at Kay's and parked in front of her house was a blue police car. "Kay's in trouble," Henry shouted, breaking into a run. "Let's see what's wrong!"

The others followed as fast as they could. I hope, Violet thought, that Kay is all right.

When they entered the house Kay was in the dining room answering a policeman's questions.

Benny dashed over to the desk where papers were scattered about helter-skelter. The floor was littered with books and papers. "Jessie," he said with his arms on his hips, "look at this mess."

Aunt Jane came over to the children and explained in a quiet voice, "Last night, Willie let out a terrible yowl. Kay and I jumped out of bed to see what was wrong and this" — she threw out her hand in the direction of the desk — "is what we found."

"Was it a prowler?" Jessie asked.

"Yes," Aunt Jane answered, with a worried frown. "We called the police about two o'clock and they came right over to search the grounds, but unfortunately they didn't find a soul. Officer Miller" — she nodded her head toward the policeman in uniform — "returned to ask Kay a few more questions."

"The prowler really tore up the desk," Henry said. "Is anything missing?"

"No," Aunt Jane responded. "Kay had some money in the bottom drawer, but it wasn't touched. Thank heavens for Willie. Evidently, whoever was searching the desk stepped on his tail in the dark."

"How did they get in?" Violet wanted to know.

"The prowler pried open a window and sneaked in that way," Aunt Jane answered.

The officer slapped shut his notebook and entered the living room.

He tipped his hat in their direction, then left.

Kay joined them, saying, "It was lucky the intruder didn't get what little cash I had." She gave them a weak smile. "Don't worry, I intend to go on fixing up my motel."

"Good," Henry said. He ran his hand through his hair. "Because I'm afraid we have more bad news for you."

Kay's green eyes darkened. "What next?" she questioned sharply.

"Millicent Fair," Jessie said briefly.

"She brought us some cookies this morning, and accidentally dropped her purse. Some letters fell out," Violet explained, "and when I picked them up, I noticed they were addressed to you."

"To me?" Kay said, a puzzled expression on her face. "Why would Millicent have my letters?"

"We think she's been taking your mail out of the mailbox," Henry said grimly. "It could be your missing reservations!"

"Oh, my," Kay said. "I can't believe Millicent is the one who has been doing all these awful things."

"Neither can I," said Aunt Jane. "Millicent was always so pleasant. But," she added thoughtfully, "she always had a hundred questions, didn't she, Kay?"

Speechless, Kay nodded. At last she spoke. "Yes, Millicent always wanted to know my every move. I don't know much about her except that she's retired and lives on a small pension." She took a deep breath. "Millicent used to work as a secretary for the Adventure Hotel chain."

CHAPTER 12

The Capture

"Isn't that the hotel trying to buy your motel?" Henry asked, frowning.

"Yes," Kay said. "I knew of her connection with the hotel, but didn't let myself think about it. I didn't see how Millicent could be the one. I think, though, now is the time to ask Millicent a few questions!" She turned and smiled at Violet. "You're a good detective, my dear."

"Shall we run and tell Millicent that you want to talk to her?" Benny wanted to know.

"Tell her to come up for coffee and rolls,"

Kay said. "Maybe, then, she won't be suspicious."

"I have the feeling she might be gone," Jessie said quietly.

"Rolf is coming to finish the roof," Kay said. "I'll talk to him about it. I really don't want to call the police again. Not until we're sure about Millicent." She turned to Benny. "Go ahead and bring her here, Benny."

"We'll see if she's in," Henry said, moving to the door.

The four Aldens left, racing downhill.

Benny was the first at Millicent's door. He knocked and knocked.

"No answer," Jessie said. "It's just as I thought."

Benny knocked louder.

"I'm afraid you're right, Jessie," Violet said.

"All right," Henry said. "Let's spread out and try to find her."

Three painters, who were finishing the trim on the windowsills, waved to Henry as he went by. One said they would soon be gone for good. Willie was weaving through the painters' legs and they tried to shoo him away.

They searched everywhere, even in the painters' truck and the bike shed, but Millicent wasn't in sight.

Discouraged, the children met back in front of their motel unit.

"From Kay's house, we had a good view of the motel," Henry said.

"That's right," Violet said. "No taxis drove in."

Jessie shook her head. "Where can she be?"

The two lanky painters walked by on the way to their truck. "Good-bye, kids. We're finished."

The third painter stayed behind. He must be new, Henry thought. And he's so plump and short.

"Let's return to Kay's," Jessie said wearily. "She'll be disappointed that Millicent has disappeared."

All at once the painter in the background sneezed — three small sneezes. Violet stared at the painter who was attempting to push Willie away. "That painter," said Violet, "sneezes just like Millicent sneezes."

All eyes turned on the plump painter in the white overalls and billed cap who was walking rapidly in the opposite direction.

"Just a minute!" Henry shouted, dashing in front of the painter and blocking his way. "We want to talk to you."

The painter sidestepped Henry, but Jessie rushed forward and grabbed his arm. The painter yanked Jessie's hair.

"Ow!" Jessie yelled, loosening her hold.

The painter twisted free, but as he did his cap flew off, revealing mussy gray hair and an angry round face.

"It's Millicent!" Benny yelled. "Stop her!"

But Millicent rushed off. She pushed Violet, causing her to topple over. Benny, feet firmly planted, stood in her way and Henry grabbed her. She gasped for breath and held up her hand. "Stop," she whispered. "I give up. I've had enough of this."

Henry hoped Millicent wasn't hurt. It was hard to believe that this sweet woman had caused Kay's problems.

Benny stared at her. "Millicent," he said

reproachfully. "Did you do all those mean things?"

Millicent just shook her head.

"Kay wants to talk to you," Violet said quietly.

"Very well," Millicent said meekly. "May I change out of these ridiculous overalls?"

"We'll wait outside your door," Jessie said, not unkindly.

In a little while, Millicent, her hair neatly brushed, came out. She wore a fresh pink dress and carried her purse, looking very different from her painter disguise.

"Let's go," Millicent said calmly.

They climbed the hill to Kay's house. The Aldens were eager to hear Millicent's explanation.

When the Aldens and Millicent arrived at Kay's house, Rolf met them and led them into the living room. Quietly the children seated themselves next to Aunt Jane. Once Millicent was settled in an easy chair by the window, Kay handed her a cup of coffee.

There was an awkward silence as Millicent nervously cleared her throat. "I-I'm sorry for what I did to you, Kay." She blinked rapidly. "You've been good to me, and I've repaid you by doing terrible things!"

"All of us want to understand, Millicent," Kay said gently. "I think we deserve to be told the truth."

Millicent nodded several times. She began in a trembling voice. "As you know, Kay, I once worked for the Adventure Hotel chain as a secretary." She sipped her coffee and went on in a stronger voice. "The hotel desperately wanted to buy the Cypress Motel so they could build a big new hotel. Mr. Warner, the manager, promised me a large sum of money if I would help them out and force you to leave." She dabbed at her mouth with her napkin.

"I knew it was wrong, but I needed the money badly. Besides, I thought you'd be happier with all the money the hotel would pay you, Kay. You could leave this old run-down motel a wealthy woman." She hesitated, looking at the Aldens. "I had no idea the motel could be changed into such a pretty place or that it meant so much to you."

Rolf leaned forward and said in a calm voice, "You damaged the shingles."

"And you turned on the running water," Jessie accused. "That really could have flooded the motel."

"Oh," Millicent said, her usual smile returning. "I didn't want *that* to happen, Jessie. I just wanted a little water in your room."

Kay refilled Millicent's cup, and the older woman gave her a grateful look.

"How did you know how to turn off the lights and water?" Kay questioned.

"Mr. Warner at the hotel told me what to do." Millicent sighed. "I surprised myself. I didn't know I was capable of some of the things I did."

"You did awful things," Kay said sternly.

"How did you end up in a painter's uniform?" Henry asked.

"Oh, I became a good liar, too." Millicent set her cup down. "But I didn't like what I was doing. I told one of the painters that I wanted to play a practical joke on you, and I asked to borrow a pair of overalls. He thought it was funny and gave me an extra uniform he kept in his truck. I was going to ride out of here with them."

"And why did you enter Kay's home and mess it up?" Aunt Jane asked.

"I was looking to see if you had any money in the house. Without money, Kay, I didn't think you could go ahead with remodeling. That wretched cat tripped me up twice. He scared me half to death when I stepped on him. I couldn't get out fast enough." She paused to remove a hanky from her sleeve. "The second time Willie tripped me up was when he uncovered my disguise by causing me to sneeze." She looked at Violet. "I saw how suspicious you were and knew I had to get away."

"You even had the nerve to dump the oranges in the pool," Violet said. She hated to believe someone she had liked and trusted could do such mean things.

"I must admit," Millicent said, "that I couldn't think up all these destructive things alone. Most of them were Mr. Warner's plans."

Jessie asked, "Where is Mr. Warner?"

"He works in the Adventure Hotel office in downtown Lyndale," Millicent said. "He came over and put the six cans of paint in the car and also carried the orange baskets down to the pool."

Behind her, Kay reached for a pad and pencil on the desk to jot down the name.

"The worst thing," Rolf said, "was stealing the six cans of paint and ruining the shingles. It was expensive."

Millicent gazed at her hands. "I'm not proud of what I've done." She looked up. "I thought if I got rid of the paint, you'd stop." Tears glistened in her eyes. "Before you call the police, I just want you to know I'm sorry, Kay." Her gaze shifted to the Aldens. "I apologize to all of you." She gave Benny a trembling smile. "I really did enjoy baking for you."

"I enjoyed eating it, too," Benny admitted. He felt unhappy at the thought of Millicent in jail.

"I'll try to repay you for all the damage I cost you, Kay," Millicent said.

"No," Kay said firmly. "I mean to have a

little chat with Mr. Warner. I'm certain the hotel will be happy to pay damages rather then risk bad publicity."

Millicent's smile returned. "Oh, what a good idea."

Kay cleared her throat. "Millicent, I'm not calling the police. I don't want to prosecute you because I think you've suffered enough."

Millicent gave a sigh of relief.

"But," Kay continued, "I think you should leave at once."

"You're not sending me to prison?" Millicent's face lighted in wonderful disbelief. "Oh," she said, "I promise to leave today, Kay. Believe me, I'll never become involved in anything dishonest again." She fumbled in her purse. "Here are the reservations." She handed Kay a bundle of letters. "You'll have plenty of tourists to keep your motel occupied all winter."

"Where will you go, Millicent?" Kay asked.

Millicent answered slowly. "I have a sister in Cleveland. I'll stay with her until I find a job." She stood up. "I'm still a fine secretary, you know. I *know* I'll find a job."

With her hands on the doorknob, she turned. A tear rolled down her cheek. "I really was fond of all of you," she choked.

Willie padded into the room. Suddenly Millicent sneezed. Three small sneezes. "That's my cue to leave," she said. She smiled weakly, and quickly left, shutting the door behind her.

The only sound in the room was Willie's purr as he settled in Violet's lap.

Finally, Aunt Jane broke the silence. "Tomorrow we must return to Greenfield, too, Kay. The children need to get ready for school, and I need to return to Andy. My husband misses me," she said with a smile, "and I miss him also."

"Not so soon!" Kay protested.

Aunt Jane laughed. "You'll do fine now. And we'll be back, won't we, children?"

"Yes," Violet said, and the others nodded enthusiastically.

"Then tonight we'll have a party to celebrate," Kay pronounced.

"Oh, boy, a party," Benny said.

"I'll bring steaks," Rolf offered.

"We'll bring broccoli," Jessie said.

"And potatoes," Henry said.

"And ourselves!" Benny said in a loud voice.

"Oh," Kay said. "Invite Catherine, too, will you?"

"With pleasure," Violet said.

For their last night, they dressed in their best. As they left unit number one a yellow taxi was leaving. Millicent was on her way.

Going up the hill, they talked and laughed. How good it was to have the mystery solved.

When they arrived at Kay's house, they were all, including Catherine, seated about a round table. Rolf brought in the steaks.

"Here they are!" Rolf boomed, dishing up a beautiful charcoal-broiled steak at each plate. He sat down next to Kay.

"Well, children," Kay said, beaming at them. "You and Jane convinced me to stay and I've never been happier."

"Yes," Jessie added. "This place is too beautiful to leave."

Kay chuckled. "*Now* it's beautiful. Thanks to your hard work."

"There were lots of mean things that happened," Benny said, helping himself to the broccoli. "I was scared once or twice."

"Yes, Benny, there were lots of bad things," Rolf said emphatically. "But they're all over now!"

"We even suspected you," Violet admitted, glancing at Rolf.

"Me?" Rolf's black brows shot up. "Oh, I see. When you didn't know who the guilty one was, you were suspicious of everyone."

Jessie smiled. "Yes, everyone." She gave a sideways glance at Catherine.

"Not me!" Catherine said, her dark eyes sparkling with humor. "I wondered myself who it could be." Catherine looked especially pretty tonight in a soft yellow dress.

Jessie gave an embarrassed little laugh. "I have to tell you, Catherine, that when we made up your bed I knocked a book to the floor and your map fell out."

Catherine said, "And you saw the big red circle around Kay's motel, and the Adventure Hotel, right?"

"Yes," Jessie said. "We wondered why."

"Because," Catherine explained simply, "this was the map I used to come to Florida. I marked Kay's motel and the hotel because I wasn't sure which one I'd stay at."

"Oh," Jessie said, laughing with relief.

"It's over now," Kay said. "I've gone through the reservations, and my motel will be occupied most of the winter."

Rolf reached over and covered Kay's hand with his big tanned one. "That's wonderful, Kay. I must admit I wanted you to sell because I thought your motel was making you unhappy. I can see now that it's just the opposite. But running a ten-unit motel will need a lot of work." He gave her a lopsided smile. "And I'll be here to help."

Benny poked Henry, grinning and motioning at Rolf.

"Won't your regular Snowbirds be surprised when they see the changes you've made?" Jessie asked.

"They'll be delighted!" Kay answered. "Excuse me," she said, pushing back her chair and going into the kitchen.

Henry and Violet cleared the table.

Kay reentered with a large cake. On the frosting were four figures outlined in pink icing, and underneath were the names Henry, Jessie, Violet, and Benny. "This is to thank you for your work and to thank your Aunt Jane for bringing you to visit me." She cut big slices for each one.

Benny's eyes grew big. "A chocolate cake!"

"Yes," Kay said, putting the pieces on plates. "A chocolate cake with fudge filling."

The night was one of happiness and laughter.

The next day as Rolf and Kay drove the Aldens and Aunt Jane to the airport they were all sad to say good-bye to Florida. Kay was sad to see them go. They were pleased, though, that Kay was happy with her motel and best of all that she had a good friend in Rolf. They would come back. Aunt Jane had promised. And they were happy another mystery had been solved.

GERTRUDE CHANDLER WARNER discovered when she was teaching that many readers who like an exciting story could find no books that were both easy and fun to read. She decided to try to meet this need, and her first book, *The Boxcar Children*, quickly proved she had succeeded.

Miss Warner drew on her own experiences to write each mystery. As a child she spent hours watching trains go by on the tracks opposite her family home. She often dreamed about what it would be like to set up housekeeping in a caboose or freight car — the situation the Alden children find themselves in.

When Miss Warner received requests for more adventures involving Henry, Jessie, Violet, and Benny Alden, she began additional stories. In each, she chose a special setting and introduced unusual or eccentric characters who liked the unpredictable.

While the mystery element is central to each of Miss Warner's books, she never thought of them as strictly juvenile mysteries. She liked to stress the Aldens' independence and resourcefulness and their solid New England devotion to using up and making do. The Aldens go about most of their adventures with as little adult supervision as possible — something else that delights young readers.

Miss Warner lived in Putnam, Connecticut, until her death in 1979. During her lifetime, she received hundreds of letters from girls and boys telling her how much they liked her books.